Lisa M.Cottrell-Bentley

Wright on Time: Minnesota

Illustrated by Tanja Bauerle

Printed in the United States of America

First Printing, 2012

ISBN: 978-1937848026
ISBN-13: 1937848027
Library of Congress Control Number: 2012943218

Do Life Right, Inc.
P.O. Box 61
Sahuarita, AZ 85629

Visit www.WrightOnTimeBooks.com to order additional copies
or e-mail sales@wrightontimebooks.com to inquire about bulk
discounts.

Dedicated to **Tanja Bauerle**
who is able to take my writings
and turn them into beautifully illustrated
characters the whole world can see and relate to

MINNESOTA

Minnesota became a State on May 11th, 1858

Common Loon
State Bird

Giant Beaver
Unofficial
State Fossil

Norway Pine
State Tree

Pink & White Lady Slipper
State Flower

Lake Superior Agate
State Gemstone

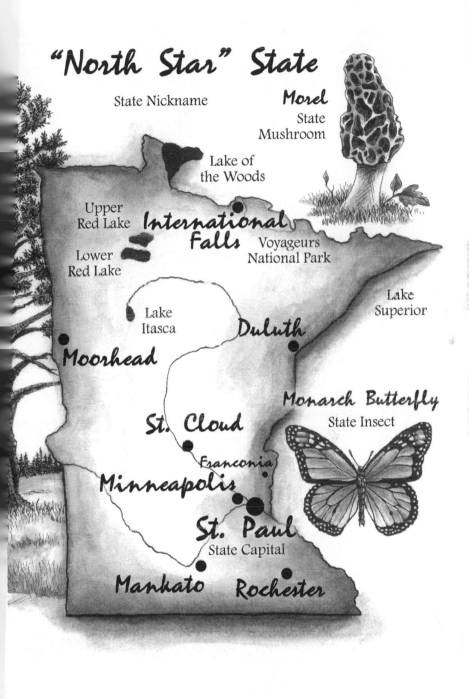

"North Star" State

State Nickname

Morel
State
Mushroom

Lake of
the Woods

Upper
Red Lake

Lower
Red Lake

International
Falls

Voyageurs
National Park

Lake
Itasca

Duluth

Lake
Superior

Moorhead

Monarch Butterfly
State Insect

St. Cloud

Franconia

Minneapolis

St. Paul
State Capital

Mankato

Rochester

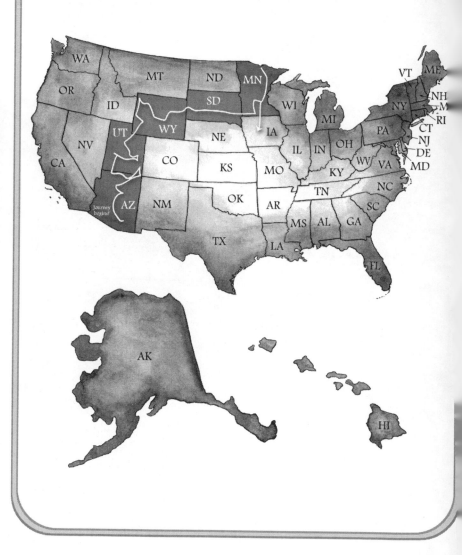

Nadia's Journal

September 21st

I'm finally starting to get used to living in an RV. Four months ago, when Mom and Dad and Aidan and I first set out on this trip, I had no idea how much we'd discover.

We started in Arizona, where we'd been living. My family and I were excited to get on the road. The very first day of our adventure, we explored a cave and found minerals, bats, and even a weird black and bronze device with a turtle pictogram on it.

After a month of exploring our home state, we drove north to Utah, where we helped out at a dinosaur dig. We uncovered fossils, Aidan lost two teeth, and I met a linguist who helped me decipher some of the glyphs on the mysterious device. I'm still researching the others. There's a bird which means 'travel', a spiral meaning 'time', and one symbol, *tun*, means 'year'. That's when we named the device the Time Tuner.

The Time Tuner started doing strange things that night. It made computers around it become fully charged and connected to the Internet. It glowed in the dark. New buttons that look like the pause, play, rewind, and fast forward buttons on a DVD player even appeared, just for a bit. Maybe it's a stopwatch? I don't know.

Next, we visited Wyoming. Yellowstone National Park was beautiful, but after the RV broke down there, Aidan and I got bored being cooped up, so Mom and Dad found new things for us to do. I loved seeing geysers and learning how to get geothermal energy. We also toured a hydroelectric dam and a wind farm. It's amazing how many sources of energy there are! Dad even wrote an article about it. I love that he writes articles about places that we go to.

At the wind farm, the Time Tuner got rain and mud on it. I was so worried it might break, but instead, it changed colors and got even more new symbols. The coolest part, though, was when plants appeared and grew at super speed— just by getting a little mud on the Time Tuner while we were thinking about specific plants. I've been trying to replicate this, but no luck yet. I think it might be coincidence or something, especially the plant part. We all think that was pretty crazy.

After Wyoming, we went to South Dakota last month. We saw the Black Hills and a few other landmarks. Prince Pumpkin the Third, our super-duper adorable little turtle, gave us a scare. We thought he was dead on our first morning there, but he ended up being better than ever, and I'm so glad we were wrong! Prince Pumpkin the Third had been standing on the Time Tuner, and it again had a new symbol. It's always giving us new mysteries to solve. I'm determined to solve them!

We got a surprise visit from Grandpa and Grandma! Seeing them makes me feel more at home even in a new state. We used to see them every few days when we lived in Tucson, and I miss them so much. In South Dakota, we all hunted for Black Hills gold, found out how newspapers are made all the way from writing to printing, and visited a motorcycle rally. At the rally, the Time Tuner did the strangest thing yet. I'd been rubbing it like a worry stone, and Mom, Dad, Aidan, and I had been holding hands—and time stopped. Yeah, seriously, it just plain stopped. Everything and everyone except the four of us just froze in place. It seems like we gave the Time Tuner the perfect name!

I'm going to experiment even more with the Time Tuner. It's still powering computers without us having to do anything, but I want to get it to grow plants or stop time again. Meanwhile, we're in Minnesota. We've seen lakes and twine balls and sculpture parks, oh my! The twine thing was Mom's idea, for her birthday, and cooler than I expected. All the art we've seen has given me an idea: I'm going to paint my space of the RV.

Chapter One

"What else would you like to buy?" Nadia's mother, Stephanie, asked her as the two strolled down another Target aisle.

The Wright family was just outside of Minneapolis, Minnesota, staying at a campground in a suburb. It was late September and their month-long Minnesota adventure was nearing its end.

"Why aren't you in school today?" a Target sales clerk in the home improvement department pleasantly asked eleven-year-old Nadia.

Nadia flipped her long red hair over her shoulder and gave the woman a winning smile. "I *am* in school."

The woman looked puzzled.

"I'm a homeschooler, and I'm always in school because life is school. I learn everywhere I go," Nadia said.

"Oh," the woman said. "Well, you'll be pleased to know we are still having our 'Back to School' sale. Or, I suppose in your case it would be a 'Not Back to School' sale. All school supplies are ninety percent off. Today's the last day and we've just about run out. Looks like you've got the last of the really good stuff."

"We're here to buy more notebooks and art supplies," Nadia told her as she pointed to their nearly full cart. "But I haven't been able to figure out what paint colors to get. We're going to paint my room!"

"Feel free to take as many color samples as you'd like," the woman said.

MINNESOTA

"Thanks!" Nadia said as the woman walked away.

Stephanie turned to her daughter and laughed. "Your *room*, huh?"

"I know, I know, it's just a bed, but it has walls around it and a ceiling. I'm going to paint it all up!"

The Wright family consisted of Nadia, her mother and father, her seven-year-old brother Aidan, and their turtle, Prince Pumpkin the Third. They had been living in a recreational vehicle for four months, traveling around the United States. They thought they'd be on the road for about two years, maybe longer.

Stephanie, Nadia's mom, telecommuted as a software engineer. Harrison, her dad, worked as a freelance writer. The two children enjoyed traveling and learning about the country they lived in. They'd been to five states so far, and it was interesting and sometimes surprising to see how different—and how similar—they were. They were all excited at the idea of seeing more of their beloved country.

After nearly five months in their RV, though, it was time to start turning it into a customized home. It had had a motel atmosphere so far, thus the shopping trip to seek out paint and other embellishments.

In the RV, Nadia's bed was currently right above the driving cabin, as she'd moved there from the bunkbeds she'd been sharing with Aidan. She liked that she was able to close the new space off with curtains for privacy whenever she wanted. She had two large cabinets which belonged to only her. There, she stored her clothing, laptop, toys, books, and movies. A week earlier, her mom had helped her put new shelving into the cabinets. This alone made an amazing difference in clutter control. Now it was time for some color.

"Oh, look at this one, Mom." Nadia held up a dark blue paint sample.

"Pretty," Stephanie said.

"It matches your new sapphire earrings Dad gave you for your birthday last week." Nadia held the sample up next to her mother's ears. "The blue is exactly the same."

MINNESOTA

"Cool. Do you want it for your ceiling?"

"Yes, I think so. I think I'll get the glow in the dark paint to paint the stars I want, instead of stickers. That way I can paint glow in the dark messages on my walls and cabinet doors too."

"Good idea. We'd better get some sand paper to sand the doors down before we paint them."

Nadia picked out a light orange for her walls, making sure to find the environmentally friendly paint. It perfectly matched the orange sheets she already had. Her bedspread was dark blue with orange, yellow, and green planets and stars on it. The stars on her bedspread also glowed in the dark, and Nadia was looking forward to spending a night cocooned in a sea of glowing celestial objects.

"These are great purchases!" Stephanie said as they stood in the checkout lane.

"I can't wait to get started. I bet Aidan is going to want to decorate his area, too, once he sees how cool mine looks."

Driving their little silver electric car, Stephanie headed toward the campground where they were staying.

"Is there anything else you've been wanting to see in Minnesota?" Stephanie asked Nadia.

"I've really loved this state. I'm not sure I'm ready to leave yet. I knew before that it was called the 'Land of Ten Thousand Lakes', but wow, there sure are a lot of lakes here. Way more than ten thousand! It looks so different than Arizona. There are so many dark green trees, so many different kinds of trees—even in the cities, and so much grass. Canoeing in the Boundary Waters was cool, and seeing the Mall of America was fun. But, honestly, I think the best part was the Kensington Runestone Museum in Alexandria. I loved the twenty-eight foot tall Viking, too."

"I thought you'd think so."

MINNESOTA

Anyone who knew Nadia knew how much she appreciated knowing a place's history. And when that history involved ancient languages in any form, she was especially enthusiastic.

The Wright family had learned a lot about the Vikings and their early settlement of Minnesota. Many people believed Vikings were the earliest European people to settle there. There were even runes to prove it, although some people thought they might be faked. After seeing the artifacts in the museum, though, the Wrights were inclined to believe the Kensington Runestone wasn't fake—or at least not faked by the man who found them. Harrison liked to tell his family that anything was possible, even the most unbelievable.

"I love seeing runic artifacts. The stone with the carved words reminded me so much of the Native American Newspaper Rocks we saw in Arizona and Utah. But the writing was completely different than anything else I've ever seen."

"It was pretty neat, especially the huge replica they made," Stephanie added.

"Yeah, that was neat. And it gave me a new lead on the some of the Time Tuner's mysterious markings. I wonder if they're medieval Swedish…"

Chapter Two

"We're going into the city!" Stephanie announced to the rest of the family as she and Nadia returned from their shopping. "I have a surprise."

"I hope it's another huge statue!" Aidan said. "Maybe another Paul Bunyan? We've seen at least ten of those so far in Minnesota."

The Wrights had discovered that Minnesota had a lot of 'World's Largest' objects scattered around the state. They'd spent two full weeks of their time in the big state driving around seeing as many as they could find. Stephanie took photographs of every single one, no matter how normal of a huge object it seemed. People they had run into told them that between Minnesota and North Dakota, there were more world's largest statues than anywhere else on Earth.

Stephanie liked the particularly weird things. She thought anything that made a person smile and think 'Whatever gave someone the idea to make that?' was a really good thing.

Aidan's favorites were the giant statues of men. These included a fifty-five foot tall Jolly Green Giant in a town called Blue Earth that Aidan had to climb up to a platform to stand underneath, and a most impressive Paul Bunyan in Akeley—Aidan could sit in the palm of his hand! He wanted to sit there all day.

"I think we've seen enough of Paul Bunyan," Nadia said.

"No way! I want to see another!" Aidan said. "Or we could walk in his footsteps again. That was freaky awesome, even if they were just part of a parking lot."

"Yes, it was," Nadia laughed. "Is it another world's largest animal, Mom?" She tugged on her mom's sleeve. "I love those as much as Aidan loves Paul Bunyan!" Nadia loved all the world's largest animals that were in Minnesota, especially the fish and birds.

"I'm hoping it's the world's largest hammock. Does that even exist?" Harrison asked with a grin. "It would be even more relaxing than the giant green Adirondack chair we saw in St. Paul."

"Nope!" Stephanie said. "Not another Paul Bunyan, animal, nor a chair," Stephanie informed them. "I think you are going to love it though."

"A giant plane?" Harrison asked with a wink as he washed another bowl in the sink. "My brother, Crash, would sure like to see those photos."

"We'll definitely get another picture of a giant plane before we leave Minnesota, but probably not today," Stephanie said.

Besides all the big things, the Wrights all particularly appreciated the parks full of art that they had found in Minnesota. They had visited sculpture parks in the towns of Vining and

Franconia, as well as the Caponi Art Park outside St. Paul.

"Where're we going then?" Nadia asked, as she put the Target bags on the table.

"Grab your jackets and the camera," Stephanie said, "and you'll soon see. It's my birthday month, and I've just realized we are a mere tiny little drive from something I've been wanting to see for a long, long time."

"But we've already seen the 'World's Largest Ball of Twine Rolled by One Man'," Harrison said with a laugh, remembering Stephanie's quest to see the twine in Darwin earlier that week.

"Yes, that was fantastic! But this'll be cool too," Stephanie said. "I promise."

"I can't wait," Aidan said. His shoes were already on and he was raring to go.

Harrison looked up from the last of the breakfast dishes and wiped the counter down. "How did the shopping go?" he asked.

"Fantastic!" Nadia said. She rummaged through their bags and pulled out a paintbrush. "I'm painting later today, or maybe tomorrow. I'm completely redecorating my cubby."

MINNESOTA

"I can't wait to see what you've picked out," Harrison said.

"Did you get more notebooks?" Aidan asked.

"Loads, and crayons and markers too. This is the best time of year to buy fun supplies. They're all on sale!" Nadia said, showing off the goodies.

"That's great," Harrison replied, hanging up the dishtowel to dry.

"Blow Prince Pumpkin the Third a kiss and let's get going," Stephanie said.

The three couldn't wait to see what Stephanie wanted to do, so they hurried and got in the car.

After a short drive, the Wright family drove up to the Walker Art Center and Minneapolis Sculpture Garden. They all agreed that this was a perfect surprise; they were excited by the idea of seeing a sculpture garden full of works by famous artists. The ones they'd seen so far were fabulous, but didn't have any sculptures by people that they had heard of before.

A warm late-summer breeze teased the Wrights. The coming fall could be seen in the changes to the plants and in the cool early morning weather, but this mid-day was perfect.

They parked their car in a parking garage, left their jackets in their car, and enjoyed the short walk to the sculpture park on this sunny, cloudless day.

Once they crossed a rather busy street and walked down some concrete stairs into the expansive park, Aidan ran ahead. He'd seen the wide grassy area, and viewed it as an open invitation. He loved to run and play, especially in areas new to him.

"Wait up!" Nadia called.

Aidan was running around in circles on the lush manicured lawn. "Check out this huge face—er, rather, lips and a chin," he said.

Aidan stopped to point at a large, bright white sculpture of half of a face. A dark bronze sculpture of a rumpled raincoat with nobody inside was behind it. An unshapely torso with legs stood to the right.

"These are officially weird," Nadia said.

"But also freaky cool," Aidan added.

"True," Nadia agreed.

"I want to see if the rest of the face is hiding somewhere!" Aidan said.

MINNESOTA

The family continued strolling around the park. The grounds were impressive, yet no one was there on this quiet weekday morning. Aidan found a statue of a rabbit jumping over a large bell. He pretended to be a bunny, hopping around and around on the grass.

"Hop, hop. Hop, hop. What do bunny rabbits say?" he asked.

"They just sort of move their noses," Nadia said.

"I don't think they really make much noise at all," Harrison said, catching up with the kids.

"I think 'Hop, hop' works," Stephanie said, snapping a photo of Aidan hopping like a bunny with the statue in the background.

The Aidan-bunny rounded a bend and his family followed him. He looked up—and stopped hopping. All their attention was caught by a huge white shape flanking a pond.

Chapter Three

"Wow!" Stephanie said. "It's so much more impressive in person."

"Freaky awesome!" Aidan said.

"Yeah, wow!" Nadia said. Both their voices were hushed in awe.

"Here's your camera." Harrison handed his wife her camera from the bag he had been carrying on his back.

"Thanks." Stephanie took the camera and immediately started lining up shots.

The object in front of the Wright family was a fifty-two foot long, twenty-nine foot high bright white spoon, with a glossy red cherry on top. The arm of the spoon bridged in a smooth arch across a small pond.

"A spoon?" Nadia finally asked. "Who would have thought to make a sculpture out of a spoon and a cherry?"

"Spoon!" Aidan hollered. "I bet The Tick would love this." Aidan was a huge fan of comics and The Tick and his sidekick Arthur were two of his all-time favorites.

His family laughed and agreed. The Tick's battle-cry was "Spoon!", so how could he not love a giant spoon?

"Well," Harrison said, still chuckling, "the plaque here says it was created by the husband-and-wife artist team of Claes Oldenburg and Coosje van Bruggen."

"It's certainly unique!" Stephanie said.

"How much does it weigh?" Aidan asked.

"Over seven thousand pounds," Harrison replied, continuing to read the sign.

"Look! It's a fountain too," Nadia said.

MINNESOTA

The family stared at the sculpture. A light covering of water gave the cherry a shiny appearance, and a huge spray of water shot out of the top of the cherry stem. A faint rainbow could be seen in the glittering spray. The whole thing had the appearance of hovering over a pond shaped like a linden seed pod. The Minneapolis Basilica could be seen in the distance.

"What's it made of?" Nadia asked.

"Aluminum, stainless steel, and paint. Apparently it has to be repainted every five years," Harrison said.

"That looks harder to paint than the walls and ceiling in my room!" Nadia exclaimed.

"It looks perfect right now," Stephanie said as she took off to walk around the spoon, looking for the perfect angles to shoot with her camera lens.

"What's it called?" Aidan asked.

"Spoonbridge and Cherry," Harrison answered.

"Spoon bridge?" Aidan asked. "You mean we could walk on the spoon like a bridge?"

"The arch of the spoon handle really does span over the pond!" Nadia said.

"I don't think we can actually walk on it, but it does look like a bridge, doesn't it?"

"Yes, freaky cool!"

The three followed Stephanie, admiring the fountain as they walked around the pond.

"This is so making me hungry for cherry pie!" Nadia said.

Harrison stopped, took a small blanket out of their backpack, and laid it on the ground. "I don't have cherry pie, but I did bring along some trail mix and fruit."

"What fruit?" she asked.

"Strawberries and mangoes."

"Yum! Sounds good."

Nadia joined her dad on the picnic blanket and got out the Time Tuner. Stephanie and Aidan continued to walk around the sculptures.

MINNESOTA

"While you two experiment with the Time Tuner, there's something I've always wanted to try. I think this is the perfect opportunity, if you'd like to help me out, Aidan," Stephanie said.

"Sure," Aidan replied. He wanted to do something more active than sitting around.

Stephanie and Aidan wandered away from the giant spoon.

"So, what are we doing?" Aidan asked.

"A magic trick. How would you like to hold that giant cherry?"

"Sure! How do you plan to do that?"

"It's an optical illusion. You'll see. Stand right there, okay, Aidan?"

"Okay."

The pair had walked far enough away from the spoon and cherry that the cherry appeared only as big as Aidan's head. Stephanie knelt down on the ground and looked at her camera's digital display. She shifted up and down and side to side, trying to get just the right angle.

"Now, can you turn and hold your arms out in front of you?" Stephanie asked.

Aidan stuck out his arms like he was holding an invisible baseball bat. "Like this?" he asked.

"Close," Stephanie said. "Maybe if you tilt your hands away from you more." From her perspective behind the camera, she tried to line up Aidan's hands with the big black cherry stem.

Click.

"Got it! Aidan, you're holding a giant cherry," Stephanie said.

Aidan ran over to peer at the camera screen. "Freaky cool! Can you take another picture? I have an idea."

The two of them got back into position, only this time Aidan opened his mouth like he was going to eat the cherry. Aidan made a few more faces, Stephanie made a few more suggestions, and soon they had created a whole photo-shoot full of fun and silly poses.

"I wish the cherry was real," Aidan said. "It does look tasty. Mmm, metal and paint."

Stephanie smiled. "Delicious. If you're hungry, let's join the picnic."

MINNESOTA

"Think we can try the Time Tuner again?" Nadia asked.

"We can try, but I don't know if it'll work like it did in Wyoming," Harrison replied. In Wyoming, the Time Tuner had mysteriously caused plants to grow during a rainstorm. Since then, it hadn't rained and the family had not been able to get it to do anything like that again, but certainly not for lack of trying. Nadia tried at least one new way to get it to work again every day.

Nadia munched a handful of trail mix, then walked over to the pond. She tried with all her might to keep one and only one thought in her mind: a cherry tree. The humongous cherry in front of her was making her want to eat one. She bent down to the water, dipped her finger into it, and allowed the drips to fall onto the surface of the device.

"Nothing," she called over her shoulder to her dad.

"Try the mud," he suggested.

She reached into the pond a little further, putting a dab of mud on her finger. She spread the mud over the surface of the device. Nothing happened. This was just as it had been at every lake, pond, stream, and river they'd tried it at.

She walked over to the blanket and plopped herself down, slightly dejected.

"It's just so odd," she said. "It seemed clear in Wyoming that rainwater and mud on the Time Tuner caused whatever plants we thought of to grow, but we haven't been able to recreate it. I've really wanted to make plants appear out of thin air again, especially when we've been hungry."

"It also hasn't rained once on our trip since then," Harrison said.

"True. I'm thinking it has to be actual rainwater, rather than any type of water. It makes sense that tap water and bottled water don't do anything. They've been filtered and cleaned. But lake and river water *is* rainwater, so I don't understand why they don't work."

"It doesn't make sense to me either. Have you written down every place we've tried?"

"Yes." Nadia took her notebook out of the bag and wrote down the time, date, location, and results from the 'Spoonbridge and Cherry' pond.

"We've officially tried one hundred and fifty-six places."

"Wow! That's more than I realized."

Stephanie and Aidan joined Harrison and Nadia on the blanket.

"Got your shot?" Nadia asked.

"Yep. It's awesome. We got the perfect shot of Aidan looking like he was holding the giant cherry!" Stephanie said.

"It's freaky awesome!" Aidan squealed.

"Cool! I can't wait to see it," Nadia said.

"No luck with the Time Tuner growing plants?" Stephanie asked.

"Nope."

"How about with making time stop?" Aidan asked.

"I was just about to try that again, actually, but I still don't remember what I did for sure that made it stop. This will be the two hundred and eighth attempt. I've been keeping a record of that too." She tapped her finger on her journal with her pen.

"We've all tried just about everything, it seems. Just do something random," Stephanie suggested. She set her camera down and reached out for a mango.

Nadia took the device into her right hand and held it gently. The top side was black with writing on it and the bottom side was a solid bronze. She began rubbing her thumb in circles around the middle of the device. After a minute, she started to look frustrated.

"I don't think it's ever going to work," she said.

"Try just a bit more," Harrison suggested.

She continued rubbing the device as she looked around at their surroundings. She couldn't help but think how beautiful the gardens were. Without noticing, she began to relax her hand, and the device started to slip from her grasp. She reflexively grabbed it hard and started circling her thumb again. As she glanced at the device she realized it had flipped upside down. She was now rubbing the solid bronze side. She stopped.

"Hey, guess I messed up," she said as she looked up to her family. "It flipped."

She had a smile on her face as she spoke, but then immediately the smile disappeared.

Nadia Wright's family was frozen.

Chapter Four

"Oh, no!" Nadia screamed.

The air around her was stiff with silence. When she'd accidentally stopped time in South Dakota, she'd had her family with her and she had felt safe. This time, she was completely and utterly alone. The silence had felt free when she'd had her parents at her side. Now it almost felt claustrophobic.

"Mom? Dad? Aidan? Can any of you hear me?" she asked in an anxious voice.

She glanced at the Time Tuner. The symbols on it were glowing blue, just as they had in South Dakota, when she had first paused time. The Time Tuner was stuck to her hand. It felt like an odd magnetic glue. Not truly magnetic, nor adhesive, but somehow both.

Her parents were sitting calm, eyes wide open and mouths agape. Had they been in the middle of saying something? Nadia couldn't remember what it had been.

Aidan's hand was nearing his mouth with a slice of mango. Below it, a drip of juice hung motionless in midair.

She decided to go ahead and explore a bit. Slowly and carefully, she stood, holding on to the device just in case it was her imagination that it was stuck. She headed nearer to the pond.

"Think you'll grow a plant for me now?" Nadia asked the Time Tuner. Her voice sounded louder than normal since everything else was completely quiet.

She dripped water, then mud, onto the device. Nothing happened.

MINNESOTA

She looked up. "The water from the fountain looks just like the spray paint at the Rally," she said, remembering the frozen spray paint artists at the Sturgis Motorcycle Rally when she had paused time in South Dakota.

She continued walking around the fountain, unsure what to do. She didn't want to wander too far away from her family, but she wanted to take advantage of the situation. It wasn't like they knew they were frozen in time, she justified.

Suddenly convinced, she headed in the opposite direction. Her hair streamed behind her as she picked up her pace and started running. By the time she got to the street, she was sweaty and starting to doubt herself again.

"What am I doing?" she asked aloud.

She made her way toward the parking garage and cautiously wove around the cars in the street, completely aware of the fact that they should be moving at forty or more miles per hour. Once in the garage, she made her way to her family's car and tried to open the door.

"Oh," she said. "I forgot the keys."

She stood and leaned on the car, trying to think what she should do. Her idea had been to try to send an e-mail while she was the only person moving around in time. She wanted to see whether or not her computer would even work. That had been the one consistent attribute the device had. From the moment in Utah when they'd learned of it, they realized all computers within a ten-foot radius of the Time Tuner were always at one-hundred-percent power and they were always connected to the Internet. It didn't matter what time of day it was, nor what the moon's cycle was. It always worked.

Nadia took a deep breath. "Guess I'll go back and get the keys," she said.

She walked slowly on her way back to her family, but was sure to briskly cross the street. She had to laugh at herself as she stopped at the edge of the street and looked both ways before crossing.

In front of a garden, where it felt like a labyrinth of trees to Nadia, she suddenly jumped with a startle. Something had made a noise! It sounded like a branch breaking.

MINNESOTA

Stifling a scream, she stood perfectly still. That was when she heard all three of her family members let out a loud scream of their own.

"Naaaaaaaaaaaaaaaaaaadia!" they all called, suddenly worried since she was no where in sight.

Time had restarted.

Chapter Five

When Nadia heard her name being called, she ran toward her family.

"I'm right here! I'm right here!" she yelled, desperate to reassure them.

Stephanie, seeing Nadia running toward them, jumped up and sprinted to her. Running every day gave Stephanie quick reflexes and she often put them to good use in parenting. But she'd never had a child literally disappear in front of her eyes before, and fear made her run faster than ever.

"Oh, Nadia," Stephanie said with a tear in her eye as she stroked her daughter's hair. "I know you are fine. I know you just must have gotten the Time Tuner to work, but oh! You…"

"You scared the daylights out of us!" Harrison said as he caught up to them.

Aidan was right behind. "It must have worked!" he said.

"It did work," Nadia said proudly. She quickly told them of her adventures. "I'm not sure why it stopped working, but…"

"But?" the three asked.

"But I'm pretty sure I know how I activated it." Nadia went on to tell them how she believed they'd been holding the Time Tuner upside down. "I want to write down my findings, but then I want to try again," she said, moving toward her notebook.

"Great idea," Harrison said. "But this time, we're all doing it."

"Agreed," Nadia said.

MINNESOTA

They made their way back to their blanket and sat down. They were happy there was no one else in sight. Nadia jotted down what had happened to her in her notebook. She quickly told her family how she thought it had all occurred.

They got in the same U-shape they'd been in in South Dakota, when time had stopped for them the first time. Aidan was sitting on the far left, next Stephanie, then Harrison, and Nadia last, so her right hand could be free to use the Time Tuner. They all waited for Nadia to do her magic.

Nadia held the device bronze side up, twirled her thumb around three quick times—and nothing happened. She sat silent.

"What's wrong?" Aidan asked, not knowing if he should let go of hands or not.

"It didn't work," Nadia said.

"Did you do *anything* else last time?" Harrison asked.

She thought for a moment. "Yes, I did. I thought I was about to drop it, so I squeezed it."

Checking to see that everyone's hands were still grasped, she quickly replicated her accidental actions. After three quick thumb rotations, she squeezed tight.

It worked. Time stopped for everyone and everything except the Wrights. They knew it immediately since the world went silent. All the traffic and bird noises just disappeared.

"Look at the fountain!" Aidan said.

"It's the silence that is really amazing," Harrison said.

"Oh, and I forgot my camera again. Next time we do this, I'm on the end," Stephanie said with a laugh.

"Thinking about next time already, are you?" Harrison asked her as he, too, laughed.

The whole scenario was astounding.

"Why did we decide to sit while we did this?" Harrison asked. "Trying to stand up while holding hands is a bit difficult."

"It sure is," Stephanie said as she wiggled to standing.

"I'll write this all down when we're done," Nadia said. She'd become a serious scientist regarding the Time Tuner.

MINNESOTA

Just as the family started to walk, time started again.

"I didn't let go this time," Aidan said. "I swear!"

"No, you didn't," Stephanie agreed.

"I thought for sure that was why time started again last time. The link had been broken," Nadia said.

"I thought so too," Harrison agreed. "No matter, let's try it again!"

The family tried it several more times, each with the same result. Nadia diligently wrote down the circumstances for every try. On the seventh attempt, she thought she had the reason.

"It has to do with how many times I rotate my thumb in a circle. It has nothing to do with a broken link between us," she announced. "At least, that's what I think."

"Let's test that idea," Harrison said.

"Yes, let's!" Aidan agreed.

They first tried having Nadia rotate her thumb two times. They then had her rotate her thumb four times. Just as Nadia had suggested, four circles seemed to pause time for twice as long as two.

"All right. This time, I am going to rotate my thumb seven times before I squeeze the Time Tuner. Once time is stopped, let's all try letting go of each other," Nadia said authoritatively.

"Okay," Stephanie agreed, "but only your dad and I will let go of hands. That way I'll be with Aidan and your dad will be with you."

"Works for me," Nadia agreed.

She stroked the device in seven quick circles, and then squeezed it tight. Time froze just as they thought it would.

"Okay, now is the time. Aidan, don't let go of Mom's hand," Nadia said. "Now!"

Stephanie and Aidan were free of Harrison and Nadia. Time was still frozen for the whole family.

"Woo-hoo!" Aidan hollered in joy.

"Now let's try having Dad and me let go," Nadia said.

She saw her mother's worried look.

"I did it once already today," she reminded her mom.

"All right," Stephanie agreed.

MINNESOTA

Harrison and Nadia let go of each other's hands. All was still stopped except the family.

"Woo-hoo!" Aidan hollered again. "Now Mom and me!"

"Yes, try it, please," Nadia said.

Harrison nodded and smiled at his wife.

"All right," Stephanie said again. She was nervous, but as eager as the others to explore the possibilities and limitations of the Time Tuner. With a deep breath, she cautiously let go of her son's hand.

They were now all four separated, and yet time was still frozen. After staring at each other for a moment, they all began exploring. Aidan looked at some ants on the ground. Stephanie grabbed her camera and started taking some photographs. She wanted to see how different things like droplets of water would look during a time pause. Nadia was pleased to see the great pictures she was getting, and she watched her mother take photographs while she pointed out more photo ideas. Harrison headed toward the water, wondering if he'd see a frozen fish. Before they knew it, time resumed.

"Again, again," Aidan said as he ran to join his family. "That was freaky awesome!"

Everyone agreed. They all wanted to see more of the paused sights.

Chapter Six

It was still early afternoon and the weather was holding. After their time-pausing strolls around the huge Minneapolis Sculpture Garden, the children wanted to go some place new. They wanted to do something hands-on and outside. Stephanie made a quick phone call, and then announced that they were off again.

"We're going back to the Franconia Sculpture Park," Stephanie told them as she headed their car onto Interstate 35 heading north. She glanced at the clock and was surprised to see how early it still was in the day. Their adventures at the sculpture garden had taken less actual time than she'd realized.

"Oh, cool," Nadia said. "I really liked that place when we went there last week."

The Wright family had visited the Franconia Sculpture Park as part of a small homeschooling tour group. They'd been amazed by the sculptures there and fascinated by how the park worked. It was unlike anything they'd ever seen or been to before. Artists and intern artists worked there for a certain length of time, each creating and helping to create unique works of art which would be on display for a few years. The works displayed were always changing.

The park was out in the country, on a large piece of land. It seemed to the Wrights that nothing else was around for miles except fields and lakes. The silence, when nobody was running powertools, was golden, and the artists there thrived in the solitude.

"I was told that Rupert Greene, one of the resident artists, will be working on his sculpture today and is looking for volunteers to help. I hope you don't mind, but I've volunteered us!"

"That's fantastic!" Aidan called from the backseat. "I can't wait to see what he's making."

"It'll be neat to know we've worked on something that thousands of people will see," Nadia said.

"That's what I'd been thinking, too, and that's why I said yes when the opportunity arose," Stephanie said, taking an exit.

The city quickly turned into countryside as they entered the scenic St. Croix valley. The family enjoyed watching the tall grass and tree-lined landscape as it passed them by.

"I still can't believe how many lakes there are here," Nadia said as she spotted yet another lake.

"Does that sign say Turtle Lake?" Aidan asked.

"Looks like it," Harrison agreed. "Are we close to Longville?" He got out his phone and looked at a map.

"Prince Pumpkin would so love to see Turtle Lake! We need to bring him on one of our day trips sometime!" Aidian exclaimed.

"Is it in the shape of a turtle, or do turtles live in it, or what? Why'd they name it Turtle Lake?" Nadia questioned.

"I don't know, but, no, we are not even slightly close to Longville. We're in Shoreview. That's where Turtle Lake is. I was going to tell you about what I read about Longville. In fact, I'm thinking next Wednesday we'll go there for their weekly summer turtle races, assuming they still do it. If they do, I'm going to write an article about it."

"Turtle races? How do they do that? Does everyone have a pet turtle?" Nadia asked.

"Yes, they actually race real turtles on one of their streets every summer. They rent out turtles for people who don't have one of their own."

The kids and their dad kept looking at the map on Harrison's phone and the big atlas they kept in the car as they continued driving.

MINNESOTA

A short while later, Stephanie stopped at the Chisago Lakes Area Chamber of Commerce and Information Center in Lindstrom.

"What are we doing here?" Aidan asked.

"I bet I know!" Nadia said, pointing at a miniature Statue of Liberty which was standing on a platform in front of the building. It was a bit larger than a person, but nowhere near as big as the real statue in New York. "Mom has to get a picture of every one of those we see!"

"That's right!" Stephanie said.

The family got out of the car and stretched their legs.

"Might as well check out the brochures while we're here," Harrison said. "We might find out about something we've never heard of before, or maybe a festival." His eyes gleamed at the idea, since he loved small town festivals.

Stephanie and Nadia checked out the statue while Aidan and Harrison went inside the building.

"Can I help you?" an elderly woman asked in a strong Swedish-sounding accent.

"We're traveling through the area. Can you recommend anything that is a must see or must do?" Harrison asked.

"Ooh, definitely," the woman replied.

The two went on talking while Aidan looked at maps and brochures.

"Thanks so much," Harrison replied after the lady gave him directions to her favorite restaurant in town.

"Where are you from?" Aidan piped in. "You have a freaky cool accent!"

"I'm from right here, lad. I was born and raised here. I'm of Swedish descent. You should hear people who are *actually* from Sweden. I can't talk like them at all. There were a few tourists in here earlier today who were from Sweden. They had the most beautiful accents."

"But, *you* have an accent!" Aidan said. "Like how you say the name of this town!"

"Lindstrom?" She pronounced it like Leend-stroom, in a slightly sing-songy way.

"Yes! It sounds so freaky cool."

MINNESOTA

"I guess that's just my Minnesotan accent," she replied. "We Minnesotans have our own dialect. Where are you from?"

"I'm from Arizona, but everyone says that I speak like a Midwesterner since so many people who live in Arizona aren't from Arizona, plus my Dad's from Iowa."

"Ah, on a trip, eh?" she asked.

"Not anymore! We live on the road now," Aidan said proudly. "We live in an RV."

"How fun!"

They hopped back into their car and before they knew it, they'd arrived at the Franconia Sculpture Park. As they parked their car, got out, and made their way to the back of the park where the sculptures were made, a young man with a long dreadlocked ponytail came and greeted them.

Wright ✤n Time

"You must be the Wrights," he said with a smile. "I'm Rupert Greene."

"Hi, I'm Stephanie. This is my husband Harrison and our two children, Aidan and Nadia."

"It's very nice to meet you all!" Rupert smiled at them.

"It's nice to meet you too," Stephanie said. "We're all excited to be here today."

"I was told you have been here before. Just a week or so ago, right?"

"That's right."

"Then I don't need to show you around. Let's get started on my project!"

Rupert led the family toward the far edge of a field. The tall grass came up to Aidan's shoulders. Men and women with tools and supplies walked past them, busy finishing up their own pieces before the park's annual festival at the end of September—just days away.

"Hey, Rupe," another man called. "Found ya some good helpers there, huh?"

"Yep!" Rupert called to the man.

MINNESOTA

Chatter could be heard in all directions. The atmosphere was friendly and happy and it was obvious that individual strangers had collected here with the goal of art, only to quickly discover they'd found new lifelong friends.

One person was working with a crane while another directed him. Two women in a different direction were slinging concrete. Another man was piling up bricks. Yet another woman was blending the largest palette of paints the Wrights had ever seen. Still another was wearing a large welding mask as she prepared to weld two pieces of steel together. In the distance, two more figures could be seen twisting a large strand of wire. A mesh of the wire lay near them and was covered in sod. The Wrights wondered what those people were making.

"This place looks completely different than when we were here last, even though it wasn't very long ago," Aidan said to his mom.

"That's the nature of art!" Rupert declared.

"So what are we going to be doing?" Aidan asked him.

"My work is called 'Seasonal Metamorphosis' and I'm using soldered metals, which I finished yesterday, a variety of weather-resistant fabrics, and paint. That's what you'll be helping with."

"Isn't there a famous artwork by M. C. Escher called 'Metamorphosis'?" Harrison asked, taking notes in his notebook. He didn't know where, but he was going to sell a story about all the artwork his family had visited in Minnesota.

"Yes, there is. The metamorphosis process is fascinating. You'll be seeing my interpretation in just a moment."

"Why would a metal be better for Nadia than me?" Aidan asked.

"What do you mean?" Harrison responded.

"Well, you were talking about a metal-more-for-sis, and Nadia is my sister, so I wondered what metal is more for her," Aidan said, with a quizzical look on his face.

Rupert chuckled. "No, a *metamorphosis* means a change into something completely different, like how a caterpillar changes into a butterfly."

"Oh! That makes a lot more sense," Aidan said, smiling.

MINNESOTA

Rupert continued walking for a short distance then stopped in front of a jumble of metal and wood. It was thirty feet long; its ends were square, ten feet by ten feet at one end, tapering smaller at the other end.

"I'm in a bit of a rush since the festival is only two days away. We're going to finish painting today, and tomorrow I'll be using the crane to lift the work onto that," he pointed to a solid post sticking up out of the ground a few feet away.

"What is it?" Aidan asked. He turned his head sideways, trying to figure it out.

Rupert pointed at the framework. It was divided into four major sections, three small ones and one large one. "This end is the top." He pointed to the right hand side. "And that end is the bottom." He pointed to the left hand side.

"Okay," Aidan said, still confused, but taking it all in.

Nadia was silent, clearly thinking.

Everyone looked at the sculpture with their heads turned sideways.

"It snows here in Minnesota, of course. I've been checking what the average snowfall depth is, and how deep the snowdrifts here in the park get." He moved to the right hand side and gestured to each section in turn. "The top layer, the largest, represents winter. The second to the top layer is autumn. The third from the top is spring. The bottom layer represents summer."

"Sounds very interesting," Stephanie said.

"When all the snow is here, the bottom three layers will be completely covered. As it melts, the layers will be revealed."

"So you are working with nature to create your art?" Harrison asked.

"Yes, exactly. It is important to me that my work is allowed to breathe, transform, and, yes, metamorphosize as the seasons progress. The only way to truly appreciate it is to come and visit it often. And, of course, the work will be photographed regularly throughout the two years it'll be displayed. I've marked a spot on the land where I or someone else will photograph it daily at the exact same time of day."

"That sounds amazing," Nadia said, nodding her head.

MINNESOTA

"So, who knows how to use spray paint?" Rupert asked.

"Maybe a refresher course would be in order for all of us," Harrison laughed. "We're just now getting our artistic feet wet."

"I'm glad you said it that way," Rupert said. "Some people think they don't have an artistic bone in their body."

Harrison laughed.

"That's me!" Aidan said, completely seriously. "I have a humerus and a radius, but I don't have a bone called an artistic."

"He doesn't mean an actual bone called an artistic! He means it as a metaphor," Nadia laughed. "But I don't think you have one of those either."

"But it simply isn't true! Everyone just has to find their own inner artist and believe in it. Everyone creates art in their own way. Some people, like me, need to build our art. Others, like engineers and mathematicians, need to create their art on paper through formulas and computer programming. Then, there are people who do their art through physical activities like sports. It's all creative and I believe it is all a type of individual art."

"Really? Because I'm really good at basketball and baseball," Aidan said.

"Cool then, bud. You're an artist!"

"And Nadia is good with words and symbols."

"Then she's an artist too!"

"I'm also about to start a painting project. I'm going to paint my area of our RV home," Nadia told him.

"That sounds fantastic! My parents always let me build whatever I wanted when I was a kid. I can really appreciate how rare their free-spirited attitude was now. All the endless hours I spent making artworks out of cardboard, recycling objects, tape, and anything else I could find were well spent. It might have seemed like bunches of mess when I was making them, but none of them were. Every single sculpture I made when I was little helped bring me to where I am today."

"Sounds like you have great parents," Stephanie said.

"I certainly do," Rupert agreed.

Chapter Seven

Rupert led them around the piece, showing the different sections in detail and demonstrating how to work with the spray paint. The paint was in big jugs on the ground with hoses attached to them for spraying. Since they were using paint that was usually meant for houses, it would hold up in the weather. Since they needed so much, little cans of spray paint weren't going to cut it for the base coats.

"Each section needs to be painted a solid color. This is where I need help. Once each section is a solid color, I'll come in and highlight some areas with accent paints of more exciting colors. See how the general shape of the design is made from metal, fabric, and wood? The paint will give the design depth. The fabric will give it flow, and the wood will give it solidity."

The Wrights nodded, taking it all in.

"So, Nadia, how about you start by painting the winter section white?"

Rupert handed Nadia the paint and showed her how to squeeze the nozzle and spray it in long, clean strokes.

"Aidan, you get the dark green for summer. Harrison, here are the orange and yellow for autumn. You'll want to alternate the colors, like camouflage. Stephanie, there is the bright green for spring." He pointed at the different jugs on the ground.

They all began painting their sections.

"I'm not sure I can do camo orange and yellow," Harrison admitted. "The colors are overlapping too much and I think I already got into Aidan's section with some yellow."

"Don't worry if the colors overlap a bit, it's all part of the metamorphosis of seasons. Once you get these sides completely painted, we'll flip it and do the last side. We'll probably have to do a little at the bottom of the two edges too."

Rupert grabbed another can of white paint, hooked up another hose, and began helping Nadia paint winter, since it was the largest section.

They each became engrossed in the project. They were silent, allowing themselves to get wrapped up in the experience. As they worked, they pushed the fabric parts of the design from side to side, in order to not soak them in paint, and reached through and around the wood parts so that they didn't miss any sections at all. By the time the first side was complete, the wood and metal of the other side looked stark and naked by comparison.

"This is exactly what I wanted," Rupert declared as he started on the accent colors on the sides. "Thanks for all your help."

"Is this turning into what you envisioned?" Nadia asked Rupert as she watched him work.

"It's very close. I had to use the materials on hand, since I didn't bring anything with me. That made it a bit more difficult. Plus, there is the time constraint," Rupert said.

"How long have you been here?" Nadia asked.

"Only a month. But I'd already drawn up all of my preliminary plans, so I knew what I wanted to create. I just didn't know for sure what materials would be available for me to use."

"What else were you hoping to add to it?" Aidan asked as he watched Rupert's swift strokes of pale green make the spring section look like it had real grass on it.

As Rupert added shading and accent colors to the sculpture, what had looked to the Wrights like simple flat metal pieces seemed to become three-dimensional objects. The Wrights stared at him as he worked, amazed at the effect of his quick painting.

"When it's done being exhibited here," Rupert told them, "I'm hoping this piece will be purchased and set up in a town square somewhere. When it is, I want to turn it into a more organic work. I want to add vines and a few trees around it so that it becomes part of the earth it is resting on."

"That sounds gorgeous," Harrison noted.

Rupert finished the highlights, then called over a group of people to help turn the large object. Together, they gently rolled it over, exposing the unpainted side that had been resting on the ground. The Wrights and Rupert finished painting the fourth side. As they worked, the seasons on the sculpture were transformed. The summer area of green grass merged into the spring flowers, which morphed into the autumn leaves, which became the winter snowflakes. Each section flowed smoothly into the next.

Each section appeared alive and fully formed, yet Rupert's expert brushstrokes had also created a blending of seasons between the sections. It was amazing how quickly it had been changed from raw metal into a work of art. The fabric on the sections, which had seemed limp and lifeless, was now alive with color.

"This went a lot faster than I anticipated," Rupert said. "I'm going to go and see if I can use the crane now. Since it's only four or so, there are still a couple of hours of daylight left."

When Rupert left, the family gathered together around the project, oohing and ahhing over its details.

Nadia took off her hat and sunglasses since the day was no longer bright and sunny. It was nearing evening and clouds were filling the sky. Aidan joined her, sipping from his water bottle.

"Did you get a snack from Mom's bag?" Nadia asked.

"Yes, you want some?"

"Please. I'm hungry!"

Aidan handed over a bag of dehydrated peas and corn for them to share.

Stephanie and Harrison walked around the long artwork. They were trying to figure out just how the wood and fabric pieces were attached. They hadn't figured it out by the time Rupert returned, driving the crane.

"We can use the crane!" Rupert hollered over the noise of the machine.

MINNESOTA

"Woo-hoo!" the kids hollered back.

"That's great!" Harrison hollered.

Rupert parked the crane and hopped out.

"I'm going to need one of you to verbally guide me, and then I'll need the other three of you to stand clear so I don't drop the sculpture on you," Rupert laughed. "We'll all have to wear hard hats, too, of course."

"I'll help," Harrison offered.

"We'll go stand over there," Stephanie said, pointing to a grassy area a good fifty feet out of the way.

"Alrighty then, let's boogie," Rupert said.

Chapter Eight

Rupert securely attached a large loop of thick rope to the top of his sculpture. He then wove the other end through the hook on the crane. The rope groaned as it settled on the hook.

Rupert hopped back into the cab of the crane and began backing it up. A loud honking noise filled the air, warning anyone behind the crane to get out of the way quickly. He continued backing up until the steel cable that held the hook was taut. At that point, he maneuvered the levers into place and began shortening the cable and raising the top end of the sculpture. Once the cable had raised it all it could, Rupert shifted more levers and lengthened the arm of the crane. He allowed it to slowly lengthen as it began to raise the art piece off the ground.

Once the crane arm was extended, the entire piece hung in the air, swaying slightly.

He called out to Harrison, "I'm going to move it over to the stake now."

Harrison followed while his family watched from a distance. Nadia was a bit fearful of really large vehicles, so this part worried her. She didn't like having her dad so close to the crane.

Rupert carefully drove the crane toward the stake. Once the crane was close, Rupert stopped. He began to shift the levers, putting the arm into position to spear the end of the sculpture onto the stake in the ground.

"Okay, let me know when I'm lined up properly," Rupert called to Harrison.

Nadia gripped her mother's hand tightly.

Harrison walked around the situation, surveying it carefully.

MINNESOTA

"Okay, you're going to have to back up about five feet and then swivel the crane's arm about fifteen degrees clockwise," he called to Rupert. "Got that?"

"Yep," Rupert said. He followed the directions Harrison gave him.

Neither man noticed the creaking noise the rope was making, but Nadia and her mother did.

"Okay, now you are going to have to raise the arm of the crane," Harrison called.

Rupert moved a lever and the arm lurched upward. As it did, the rope gave another loud creak and then suddenly snapped! The whole sculpture began to fall, right toward Harrison.

Nadia let out a scream and clutched the Time Tuner in her pocket. She had, without realizing it, been using it as a worry stone again.

Stephanie gasped, but even as she heard Nadia's scream she realized that everything else had gone silent. She and Nadia looked at each other. They were the only ones not stopped in time. They both understood the urgency of the situation. With a quick glance back at the frozen Aidan, they started to run over to Harrison.

"Help me push him out of the way," Stephanie said as she started pushing her husband.

"Let me try and add more time first," Nadia said, grasping the Time Tuner.

She'd never tried this before, but it was an emergency and she needed to try now. She quickly circled her thumb around and around, counting all the way to fifty. She hoped the circle strokes correlated to fifty minutes, but she wasn't sure. Finally, she gave the Time Tuner a squeeze.

"Okay. The Time Tuner is stuck in my hand, but I think I can still help," Nadia said.

The two slowly moved Harrison inch by inch until he was clear of the falling sculpture. They had trouble moving him in a standing position, so they carefully laid him down and moved him like they were moving a heavy table. Once he was out of the way, they left him in his prone position.

"At least he won't fall down," Stephanie laughed. Her fear was ebbing now that her husband was safe.

"We need to save the sculpture too," Nadia said.

"Yes, but how?" Stephanie asked.

MINNESOTA

The two carefully walked around, checking out their options.

"I think I should climb up there and tie a new rope between the sculpture and the hook," Nadia said.

"I agree that that is what needs to be done," Stephanie said, "but I'm the one who is going to do it."

"But I can!" Nadia said.

"With the Time Tuner on your hand?" Stephanie looked at her. "I know you could, but you need to be in charge of making sure time stays stopped while I am up there!"

Nadia thought for a second and then nodded in agreement. "Okay, let's do it."

Stephanie picked up a nearby coil of rope and put it over her shoulder. She and Nadia then climbed onto the crane. Nadia sat on the front of the machine while her mother slowly climbed up its arm. She was a physically capable woman who enjoyed rock climbing and other outdoor sporting activities, but this was completely different. The danger was more real and she was nervous. But she also knew it needed to be done, so she focused on the task at hand.

Stephanie edged her way up the side. Once at the top, she laid her body as solidly as possible on the end of the arm. She slipped the rope off of her shoulder and reached down to tie it to the sculpture.

"You have good reflexes!" Stephanie called down to Nadia. "You must have stopped time just moments after the rope snapped."

The art piece had only had time to drop a foot, so Stephanie was able to reach it without much trouble.

"Be careful up there!" Nadia called back. She'd never before seen her mother so high in the air without a harness and safety rope.

Stephanie tied the other end of the new rope onto the hook, double-checked the whole thing, and then slid her way down the crane arm.

"Well, that's on securely," she said. "I think that's all we can do."

"I think so too," Nadia agreed.

Just as they stepped off the crane, time resumed. The new rope made a loud crack as it was pulled taut. The arm of the crane bounced as it took the full weight of the sculpture again. Harrison and Rupert both let out loud yelps.

"Harrison, man, you okay?" Rupert shouted, noticing Harrison lying on the ground. "Something weird happened."

Harrison stood up, slightly dazed. He gave his wife and daughter a quizzical look. "I'm fine; just seemed to fall over or something," he said.

"So long as you're all right," Rupert said as he looked around. "Oh, man, didn't notice you two there," he said, seeing Stephanie and Nadia for the first time. "Everything okay?"

"We just noticed Harrison falling and we were checking on him," Stephanie called up to Rupert. "We'll go back over by Aidan and watch now!"

Nadia and Stephanie looked at each other and giggled as they walked back over to Aidan. They'd saved the day, but they certainly couldn't tell Rupert!

Rupert and Harrison continued the installation of the sculpture even more slowly and carefully than they had before, finishing up without further difficulties.

Chapter Nine

The Wright family and Rupert looked up at the thirty foot tall column of painted metal, festive fabrics, and weathered wood. The wind had picked up and the fabric blew, making the piece look organic and alive.

Stephanie took a few photographs. They all were enjoying the experience of having participated in putting together such a magnificent art sculpture.

Rupert walked around it one last time and declared it complete.

"I'm really happy with how it turned out," he said with a smile. "The wind is even cooperating!"

"It sure is," Harrison said. "I've even felt a sprinkle of rain!"

"Thanks so much for your help, all of you."

"It was our pleasure," Stephanie said, wiping a raindrop from her face.

"Definitely!" Aidan said. "This has been so freaky cool to do!"

Nadia was on the other side of the sculpture, not paying attention to the conversation. She had something else on her mind.

"I'm going to go put the crane back now, and invite everyone to come and see 'Seasonal Metamorphosis'," Rupert said. "I'll be back in just a few minutes."

As soon as Rupert had left with the crane, Nadia called to her family.

When they approached her, she whispered, "Did you feel the rain?"

"Yes," they said, nodding.

MINNESOTA

"Well? Should we try it?" she asked with excitement and hesitation in her voice.

They immediately understood what Nadia was proposing.

"Yes! Yes! Yes!" they all said.

Aidan started jumping up and down.

"It's what Rupert said he wanted to do eventually," Harrison said. "But we better hurry."

"He won't be gone long," Stephanie added.

"It's starting to actually rain now, this is perfect," Aidan squealed. He could barely contain his excitement.

"Climb into the middle, it's bare dirt around the stake and it seems like that would be the best spot," Harrison directed.

"Pass me the Time Tuner while you climb in," Stephanie said.

Nadia handed Stephanie the Time Tuner and climbed into the sculpture. Rainwater hit the device and it turned blue. A white pictogram appeared.

"There's that symbol again!" Nadia said.

It looked Asian or Middle Eastern to Nadia. She tried to memorize what it looked like as quickly as she could because she didn't have much time and she'd left her notebook in the car.

"We saw that in Wyoming," Stephanie said. "Now we just need to get it to turn green like it did in Wyoming. I'm not sure what caused that, but I think it was mud."

Harrison took the device and brought it up to his face to examine it closely. "I wonder what this symbol means, and what the Time Tuner does when it's in this mode?"

"Let's figure that out later, so that it doesn't do anything dangerous while we're here." Stephanie said.

"I'll take it now." Nadia reached out to her dad and took the Time Tuner.

"Do you have mud?" Aidan asked.

"No, it's not raining in here. The metal framework is keeping me dry."

Harrison looked around and spotted a plastic bowl that had been sitting on the ground. It had a tiny bit of water in the bottom.

"Here," he said as he handed the bowl through the wall. "Try this water."

MINNESOTA

Nadia took a bit of the dirt from the ground and put it into the bowl. She stirred the mixture with her finger, then took the mud that formed and wiped it onto the Time Tuner. The device faded from blue to a deep, faintly glowing green with the same crop circle symbol it had shown in Wyoming. She pressed the symbol and immediately, a green shoot sprouted through the ground.

"I can see Rupert, he's coming!" Aidan said loudly.

"Hurry," Nadia whispered to the shoot.

But it wasn't hurrying enough. She thought quickly and made a decision. She grabbed a branch of the plant with her left hand and held out the device with her right. She swirled her thumb around seven quick times and then squeezed hard. It was now or never to find out whether the growing and the time pausing could occur simultaneously.

Nadia noticed the time pausing instantly. The silence was her first clue. The rain frozen in mid-air was her second.

"I didn't realize how loud the rain was," she said to herself.

She squatted down to the ground and looked at the green shoot.

"All right, little plant, grow quickly!"

As if listening to Nadia's request, the plant grew at record speed. Nadia had to quickly slip out of the artwork so the branches wouldn't touch her. She gasped at the sight of what she'd thought would be a vine. It wasn't a vine, it was a tree! A tree that was weaving itself around the large stake in the ground. In fact, it was covering the stake's entire surface, so that the stake was actually becoming embedded into its core.

"What was I thinking about when I put mud on the Time Tuner?" she asked herself.

Within seconds, it was apparent. The tree was tall and its branches filled up the entire middle portion of the sculpture. The ends of the branches wove their way through parts of the spring section. Bright green leaves burst out and were quickly covered with fluffy white blossoms.

The fragrance was strong and filled the air.

She breathed it in deep. "I don't believe it," she said to herself. "It's a cherry tree!"

Fully formed and ripe, cherries soon began popping out on all the branches of the tree. She grabbed one and tasted it. It was the most delicious fruit she'd had in her entire life. She closed her eyes in pleasure, allowing her taste buds to enjoy the flavor as long as possible.

"Guess I still had 'Spoonbridge and Cherry' on my mind," she said once she'd finished eating her cherry.

She cleaned off the seed with the rainwater in the air and pocketed it. She then found her way to stand next to her mother and stood in silence as she waited for time to restart.

"Oh, freaky wow!" Aidan said.

Stephanie saw her daughter at her side. "Did you...?" she asked.

Nadia nodded. "And it worked! Both at the same time."

"Wow, Nadia, did you make a cherry tree?" Harrison asked.

Aidan had already picked three cherries. "Can we eat some?" he asked.

"Yes, definitely," Stephanie said.

They chewed on their cherries as Rupert and the other artists joined them.

"Oh, Rupert! It's gorgeous!" a woman declared.

"Those colors and shapes," another woman exclaimed.

"It's truly a magnificent work of art," a man stated.

"You must be so proud," the first woman said.

"I am," Rupert said as his gaze was drawn from the top of his sculpture downward.

The sun was going down quickly now and the rain was getting harder, but even in the waning light the tree was unmistakable.

"What? How?" Rupert asked as he stepped forward to touch the tree which was peeking out of his sculpture. "It's... it's..." he stuttered. "It's a cherry tree."

The Wright family smiled at Rupert as he looked from one of them to another.

"How did you do this? How did this happen?" he asked.

"Don't know," Harrison said.

Stephanie shook her head in wonder.

"It's a mystery," Aidan said.

"A perfectly glorious mystery," Nadia agreed.

Chapter Ten

"Prince Pumpkin the Third," Aidan called as the Wright family entered their RV home. "How was your day?"

"You wouldn't believe ours," Nadia said.

"That spoon!" Aidan said.

"Yeah, Prince Pumpkin, we saw a spoon that was freaky huge. It was made of metal and on the tip of the spoon was a cherry," Nadia said.

"Plus, we experimented with the Time Tuner. We got it to freeze time again, lots of times!" Aidan added.

"And Nadia and Stephanie saved my life," Harrison told the turtle. He whispered another private thanks to his wife.

"You're welcome," Stephanie whispered back as she put her arms around him.

"And I got the Time Tuner to grow a cherry tree!" Nadia exclaimed.

"It had the most delicious cherries ever," Aidan said.

"I kept a few seeds. I'm hoping to plant them at Uncle Martin's house in Iowa." Nadia pulled a handful of cherry pits from her pocket. "I can't wait to see Kestrel," she continued. "I've missed her so much!"

"We'll be there in another week," Harrison said. "Uncle Martin and Aunt Robin will be thrilled to see you kids. I got an e-mail from them this morning. Martin said your cousins can't wait to go trick-or-treating with you two."

MINNESOTA

"Trick-or-treating?" Nadia and Aidan asked simultaneously. They looked at each other for a moment, then burst into a flurry of questions.

"What will I wear?" Nadia asked.

"What will I be?" Aidan asked.

"Don't worry," Stephanie said as she put her arms around her kids. "I'm sure we'll come up with something fabulous."

THE END

GLOSSARY

adhesive [ad-**hee**-siv]; similar to glue.

aluminum [*uh*-**loo**-m*uh*-nuh*m]; a light silver colored metal.

artifact [**art**-i-fakt]; a historical object.

authoritatively [*uh*-**thohr**-i-tay-tiv-lee]; having an expert opinion on a topic.

Wright On Time

Bunyan, Paul; a larger-than-life lumberjack in North American folklore who symbolizes working hard and overcoming obstacles.

celestial [s*uh*-**les**-ch*uh*l]; having to do with the sky or heavens.

circumstance [**sur**-k*uh*m-stans]; the conditions surrounding an event.

claustrophobic [klaw-str*uh*-**foh**-bik]; feeling nervous in tight spaces.

cocooned [k*uh*-**koond**]; safely wrapped inside.

coincidence [koh-**in**-si-dens]; when two or more things happen at once just by random chance.

constraint [kuhn-**straynt**]; a requirement or limit.

decipher [dee-**sie**-fer]; to discover the meaning of something.

MINNESOTA

dejected [dee-**jek**-ted]; discouraged.

dialect [**die**-uh-lekt]; a version of a language spoken by group of people from a particular area.

diligent [**dil**-i-j*uh*nt]; persistent and direct in pursuing a particular task.

embedded [em-**bed**-ed]; enclosed within something else.

embellishments [em-**bel**-ish-m*uh*nts]; decorations on something.

flanking [**flank**-ing]; going along side of.

Franconia Sculpture Park; sculpture park open to the public in Franconia, Minnesota, northeast of Minneapolis/St. Paul.

freaky awesome, freaky cool, freaky weird, freaky wow; fun phrases Aidan Wright is popularizing. *Aidan saw a really neat object. "Freaky cool!" he said.*

Wright 🕊 n Time

freelance writer; the job of a writer that works alone and is contracted for specific writing assignments. *Harrison Wright is a freelance writer.*

glyph [**glif**]; a symbol that represents a sound or a word.

homeschooled [**hohm**-skoold]; educated at home. *The Wright children are homeschooled.*

humerus [**hyoo**-mer-*uhs*]; the bone in the upper arm, from the shoulder to the elbow.

humongous [hyoo-**mung**-*guhs*]; very big, huge.

labyrinth [**lab**-*uh*-rinth]; a huge maze for people to walk through.

linguist [**ling**-gwist]; a person who studies languages.

magnetic [mag-**net**-ik]; having properties of or acting like a magnet.

MINNESOTA

metamorphosis   [met-*uh*-**mohr**-f*uh*-sis];   a complete change from one thing into another, e.g., a caterpillar into a butterfly.

Minneapolis Sculpture Garden;   large garden in downtown Minneapolis with lots of famous sculptures.

pictogram [**pik**-t*uh*-gram]; a picture or symbol that represents a word.

preliminary [pri-**lim**-*uh*-nair-ee]; early, before the main part.

radius [**ray**-dee-*uh*s]; one of the bones of the forearm, between the elbow and the wrist; or the distance from the center of a circle to any point on the circle.

raring [**rair**-ing]; eager and excited to do something.

recreational vehicle (RV); large vehicle that people can travel and live in. *The Wright family live in an RV.*

replica [**rep**-li-k*uh*]; a copy, sometimes a different size than the original.

replicate [**rep**-li-kayt]; to make a copy of or to do again.

rune [roon]; characters in certain ancient alphabets, often carved into stone.

solitude [**sol**-i-tood]; being alone.

Spoonbridge and Cherry; famous sculpture of a large white spoon with a cherry on it. Located at the Minneapolis Sculpture Garden in Minnesota.

telecommute [**tel**-i-k*uh*-myoot]; to work at home using a computer that is connected to a company's network.

MINNESOTA

Time Tuner; amazing device the Wright family found in a salted cave in Southern Arizona, properties currently being discovered.

transform [trans-**fohrm**]; to change in form or appearance.

Walker Art Center; art center located next door to the Minneapolis Sculpture Garden.

MORE FACTS ABOUT MINNESOTA

- Highest Point: Eagle Mountain, 2301 feet above sea level

- Lowest Point: Shore of Lake Superior, 602 feet above sea level

- Size: 86,943 square miles (12th largest state)

- Residents are called: Minnesotans

- 32nd state to officially become a state

- Also known as: "The Gopher State" and "The Land of 10,000 Lakes"

- Bordering States: Michigan (in Lake Superior), Wisconsin, Iowa, South Dakota, North Dakota

- Bordering Country: Canada

- State Beverage: Milk

- State Fish: Walleye

- State Fruit: Honeycrisp Apple

- State Grain: Wild Rice

- State Motto: "L'Etoile du Nord," which means "The Star of the North"

- State Muffin: Blueberry

- State Photo: "Grace" (by Eric Enstrom in 1918)

- State Sport: Ice Hockey

- State Soil: Lester

- State Song: "Hail Minnesota"

What is the image the Wright family sees on the *Time Tuner*?

In Arizona, the Wright family found a *mysterious* device which shows an image of a turtle with a special symbol in the middle. The symbol is based off of an ancient Mayan glyph called a **Hunab Ku** symbol. The Mayans believed that the symbol represented the gateway to other galaxies beyond our own sun. Only the maker of the device understands why the Hunab Ku was drawn inside of a turtle on the *Time Tuner*. Check out **www.WrightOnTimeBooks.com** and read *Wright on Time: IOWA, Book 6* to find out more!

Join Nadia and Aidan on their first adventure in *Wright on Time: ARIZONA, Book 1*. There the Wrights explore a salted cave. Nadia hopes to find minerals and see rock formations. Aidan really wants to see bats. This is the adventure where the mysterious device is found. Where was it, and what does it do?

Join Nadia and Aidan as they continue their adventures in *Wright on Time: UTAH, Book 2*. The Wrights have joined a dinosaur dig searching for allosaurus bones. Will they find any? And what will they learn about that mysterious device?

Join Nadia and Aidan in *Wright on Time: WYOMING, Book 3*. The Wrights visit geysers, tour a hydro-electric water plant, fly in a private plane, and more! What will they find and what will they learn about that mysterious device they found in Arizona?

In South Dakota, the kids wonder what all those motorcycles are doing in the town of Sturgis. Nadia learns how newspapers are created. Aidan gets to lead the way on a daring round of follow the leader. Prince Pumpkin III, their turtle, stumbles across something that he probably shouldn't have. Meanwhile, what startling new secrets of the *Time Tuner* are revealed?

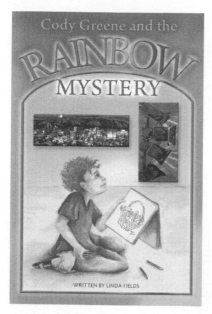

When a painting is stolen from nine year old Cody Greene's family's art gallery, he does what any artist would do: he sketches the clues. Through cooking with his friend, visiting a midwife with his mom, hiking with his dad, and helping to prepare for an upcoming art and craft festival, Cody's homeschooling takes a new turn as he unravels the Case of the Rainbow Mystery.

Write a book with Monica and Julie! When two homeschooling best friends team up to enter a novel writing contest, things get busy fast! Through planning for birthdays and getting ready for Halloween, Monica and Julie's writing adventure becomes one novel concept!

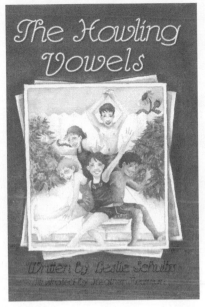

The Howling Vowels

Written by Leslie Schulz

Illustrated by ...

"Look! Five vowels, all howling!" Welcome to Sundog, Minnesota! When homeschooled, Norse-myth-obsessed Alexa Stevens moves from New York City, she doesn't know what to expect. What is a small town like? Explore a new landscape with Alexa as she observes wolves in the wild and forms a close pack of friends: Eduardo, Isabelle, Otto, and Ursula.

When mythical creatures unleash worldwide cataclysms, earth-controlling Joe rounds up super-strong Grace, information-absorbing Natalie, weather-making Valencia, and fire-starting Drake to defeat the force behind the destruction. While rebuilding their community in Sahuarita, Arizona, the team struggles to change the fate of a now fractured Earth.

FRACTURED FATE

CAJA COYOTE
SAGE ECHO SIROTKIN

ABOUT THE ILLUSTRATOR

Tanja Bauerle is an award-winning illustrator who escaped from many years in the corporate arena of design to pursue her love for children's book illustration. She has illustrated three picture books to date and is continuing to illustrate the *Wright on Time* chapter book series. Tanja is currently focusing on developing her own stories and is excited and hopeful to soon be published as both a writer and illustrator.

Originally from Germany, Tanja grew up outside Melbourne, Australia, and now lives near Phoenix, Arizona, with her husband, Kevin, her daughters, Isabelle and Zoe, her menagerie of two Golden Retrievers, three cats, six chickens and two rescued foster horses. She is a member of SCBWI and is always working on improving her skills. In her free time, Tanja loves to go kayaking and camping with her family and continues to volunteer at a local horse rescue.

www.tanjabauerle.com
Twitter: @tanjabauerle
www.facebook.com/tanja.bauerle
www.facebook.com/Tanja.Bauerle.Illustration

ABOUT THE AUTHOR

Lisa Cottrell-Bentley has been writing since she was a child, winning her first writing contest at age 9. Lisa and her daughters spent many hours searching for children's books about homeschoolers, but found very few. So, they decided to create their own. As they discussed their dream storylines, the *Wright on Time* series took shape. While they haven't found any mysterious devices yet, they have done lots of field research trying out many of the activities described in these books.

Lisa lives and learns while writing in southern Arizona (and northern California) with her husband Greg and two happy always-unschooled daughters Zoe and Teagan. Her desire is for all people to become empowered to live their own personal dreams, now and for always; she encourages this through her Doing Life Right Teleconference. Lisa also owns the Do Life Right, Inc. publishing company, which specializes in books for and about realistic homeschoolers of today.

www.WrightOnTimeBooks.com
www.DoLifeRightInc.com
Twitter: @cottrellbentley
www.facebook.com/WrightOnTimeBooks
www.facebook.com/DoLifeRightInc
www.facebook.com/DoingLifeRight (Teleconference)

NOTES:

NOTES:

Wright On Time®

Flat Aidan

Color Aidan, cut him out and take him with you.

Flat Nadia

Wright on Time®

Made in the USA
San Bernardino, CA
23 August 2014